For Mary

The Birthday Present

When she was eleven years old, Katrina Picket summoned Merlin from across a vast continent and a very large ocean. He appeared instantly, looking dishevelled, windswept and rather startled. He was holding up a long silver wand, pointing it theatrically as if he was about to do a spell. But when he saw Katrina, he hid it guiltily behind his back.

Katrina was very pleased to see him.

She was in mortal peril.

* * *

It was the thirteenth of September: the school term had started a week ago and today was Katrina's eleventh birthday.

She had set her alarm ridiculously early and had crept downstairs before it was light. It was just possible that Merlin and his dragon friend Desmond might have sent Katrina a card or a present, and if they had, she didn't want Mum to know. Mum had banished Merlin from their house at the start of the summer holidays after Katrina had accidentally woken him from fifteen hundred years' sleep. Together, Merlin and Katrina had saved Albion – or England as people called it nowadays – from total catastrophe. Mum knew nothing about Katrina's heroic exploits. She had no idea that Katrina was a sorceress and that Merlin had promised to come back and train her as his apprentice. Mum thought Merlin was an eccentric actor and had ordered Katrina to keep well away from him. She would be furious if she found out they kept in touch.

Katrina stood shivering in the hall, waiting for the postman. At last, when she'd been there so long that her skin was faintly blue and her kneecaps were bobbing up and down with the cold, some letters plopped on to the mat. Katrina gathered them up, went through to the kitchen and sat down at the table. She looked at the envelopes in disappointment. There was only one card and it was from Gran – she recognized the large, swirling handwriting. Katrina was about to open it when she heard a faint scratching sound from the front door, and the letterbox gave a small, rusty squeak. Katrina looked up just in time to see a square parcel land on the mat. She ran to fetch it, feeling very glad indeed that she had got up before Mum. The package had no stamps on, so it had clearly not come by the usual postal system.

The parcel was about the size of a thick book, and wrapped in paper that glowed iridescent green. It had spectacular pictures of flying dragons emblazoned upon it. Written on the label in purple ink were the words "To Sir Katrinapicket, with love from Merlin and Desmond."

Katrina clutched the parcel to her chest, feeling a wave of emotion wash over her.

"Sir Katrinapicket," she whispered proudly to herself. "*Sir* Katrinapicket." She'd been knighted by King Arthur after she'd saved Albion. The real King

Arthur. The thought of him made Katrina's knees feel a little wobbly. She sat down at the kitchen table and wondered where he was now. He'd planned to head off to California with Lancelot and Guinevere. Katrina missed them all. The love that had flowed between the three of them had crackled like a force field, and held everyone around them in a charmed embrace. England seemed smaller and flatter without them. She sighed. Wherever they were, she hoped they were happy.

Katrina turned her attention to the package, opening it carefully. Inside were two small presents and a postcard.

"We are staying at a place called Disneyland," she read, *"with a friendly little chap called Mickeymouse who never ceases to grin. It is quite extraordinary. Desmond is feeling very at home here. Everyone thinks he is a robot."*

Katrina smiled with relief. She was glad things were working out for Desmond. Being a real dragon, he'd had to spend years in hiding pretending to be a statue. But it seemed he didn't need to any more – he could walk about quite openly and everyone just thought he was some sort of special effect, an amazing example of modern technology.

Merlin's Apprentice

TANYA LANDMAN

Illustrated by THOMAS TAYLOR

**WALKER
BOOKS**

First published 2006 by Walker Books Ltd
87 Vauxhall Walk, London SE11 5HJ

2 4 6 8 10 9 7 5 3 1

Text © 2006 Tanya Landman
Illustrations © 2006 Thomas Taylor

The right of Tanya Landman and Thomas Taylor to be identified as author
and illustrator respectively of this work has been asserted by them in
accordance with the Copyright, Designs and Patents Act 1988

This book has been typeset in Stempel Schneidler

Printed and bound in Great Britain
by Creative Print and Design (Wales), Ebbw Vale

British Library Cataloguing in Publication Data:
a catalogue record for this book
is available from the British Library

ISBN-13: 978-1-4063-0201-1
ISBN-10: 1-4063-0201-5

www.walkerbooks.co.uk

Katrina carried on reading.

"People smile and wave and pat Desmond most affectionately. He complains that it tickles. Wednesdays are proving a little tricky, but Desmond is being very patient, although he is ravenous. Will be back to start your training once our holiday is over.

Love Merlin.

PS Desmond sends his fondest regards."

Katrina looked at the front of the postcard. There was a photo of Disneyland, and there, unmistakably, was Desmond, marching at the head of the parade with Merlin on his back waving a huge silver wand. *But Merlin doesn't use a wand,* thought Katrina. *He doesn't do spells – not like that.*

"Wands are for amateurs," she said to the photograph. "That's what you told me. What are you up to, Merlin?"

She hoped Desmond would be content to remain hungry while he was there. A few centuries ago he had eaten someone every Wednesday, but she didn't think it would go down too well with the Disneyland management if their visitors started disappearing, even if it was only once a week.

Katrina looked at the first present and laughed.

It was a pot of marmalade. Merlin adored marmalade, and it was obviously the most precious thing he could think of to send her. She was touched.

The second present was a tiny glass dragon, delicate and beautifully crafted. Katrina put it carefully beside her on the kitchen table, and felt a little lump form in her throat as she thought about Desmond. She was really very fond of him.

As she sat at the table, she heard a faint slithering sound from the front door, and another parcel plopped on to the mat.

Katrina went to pick it up, puzzled. It was smaller than the first – a thin, scarlet box about the size of an empty crisp packet – and there didn't seem to be anything written on it. As she turned it over in her hand the letter "M" rose from the box like a very faint wisp of red smoke. But when she peered at it more closely the smoke dissolved and vanished. Katrina was perplexed. It felt magical – there was a tingle beneath her fingers as she held it that couldn't be anything else. And yet it couldn't be from Merlin, could it? Why would he have sent two presents?

Katrina considered all the other people she knew

whose name began with an "M".

There was Mum – well it couldn't be from her. She wasn't even up yet, and in any case, she always waited until after breakfast to give Katrina her presents.

Mordred – no, impossible. He wasn't the type to send unexpected gifts. And anyway, Desmond had eaten him.

It had to be from Merlin: she couldn't think of anyone else who would send a parcel without using the normal postal system. Maybe he'd forgotten that he'd already sent one – he was quite often a bit absent-minded.

Shrugging, Katrina lifted the lid of the box, and gasped.

Inside was a necklace, and it was quite the most beautiful thing Katrina had ever seen.

The beads were transparent – almost like diamonds. But these weren't cold, angular stones. Curving as fluidly as droplets of water, light seemed to radiate from the heart of the beads as though they contained splinters of sunshine. Threaded together with the thinnest, most delicate strands of silver, the necklace reminded Katrina of a newly made spider's web, heavy with dew and sparkling with rainbow colours in the early morning sun. Lifting it carefully from the box, she held it up to the kitchen window. It danced with light and Katrina was enraptured.

At that moment there was a movement from upstairs: Mum was awake.

Katrina quickly laid the necklace back in its box, slipped the marmalade and the glass dragon into her dressing gown pocket, then quietly went upstairs to her bedroom.

Once there, she hid the marmalade under her bed, and put the glass dragon carefully amongst her other ornaments where she hoped Mum wouldn't notice it.

She couldn't bear to hide the beautiful necklace. Perhaps she could wear it under her school jumper. If she kept the top button of her shirt done up, Mum wouldn't see it.

Katrina was dying to see what the necklace looked like on, but there was no mirror in her room, and Mum was hogging the one in the bathroom. So instead she fastened it around the neck of her teddy bear, Bernard, so she could admire it from across the room.

As she pushed the catch home, Katrina leapt back in surprise. Her fingers were scorched – burning with pain as if she'd touched a hot saucepan. But what could she have burnt them on? Not the necklace, surely? She looked at Bernard and gulped with horror: his fur was smouldering. The beads of water had transformed into beads of fire. The sunlight contained in them was glowing a fierce, angry red, and scarlet droplets were growing into flames which started to lick about her teddy's neck. Suddenly a column of fire shot up, reducing Bernard to ashes in an instant. Katrina stifled a shriek.

"Are you all right, Kat?" Mum called from the bathroom.

"Yes," she shouted back, in as steady a voice as she could manage. Since her adventures with Merlin she didn't want to involve Mum in anything too out of the ordinary, and the Bernard bonfire was as far from ordinary as it was possible to be. Katrina chewed her lip anxiously. Perhaps it was her fault: Merlin hadn't trained her yet, after all. Perhaps she'd got over-excited about her

birthday and caused the fire by accident somehow. After all, she'd exploded a carton of orange juice when she'd got cross trying to open it earlier in the summer. Maybe the necklace disaster was just another mishap. It was possible. Wasn't it?

She swept the pile of ash into a bag and put it in one of her drawers. Then she covered the scorch mark with a book. She was trembling and shocked, but she was also very cross. She'd had Bernard since she was a baby. She'd cuddled him so much over the years that he was furless in places; he'd been one-eyed since Katrina had swallowed the other at the age of two. And now poor, balding Bernard was reduced to ashes. But still... Suppose she'd put the necklace on herself? Katrina felt a wave of cold horror sweep over her: if she'd fastened the clasp around her own neck, would the same thing have happened to her?

As she went downstairs, Katrina's stomach jiggled with anxiety. She couldn't get away from the uncomfortable sensation that something very strange was going on.

The School Trip

At school, things got worse.

By the time she'd opened the brightly wrapped gifts from Mum and Dad and her brother Adrian, Katrina was late leaving the house, so she arrived in the classroom only a minute before registration. The thought of Bernard's strange and dramatic end made her feel distinctly nervous and she hoped that school would take her mind off it. But then Daisy started to behave oddly.

Daisy had been Katrina's best friend ever since

nursery, and Mum and Dad were taking them both to the cinema after school as Katrina's birthday treat. But instead of her usual smile and friendly thump-on-the-arm greeting, Daisy gave Katrina a cold, hard stare and turned back to the magazine she was reading. She didn't even say "hi" or "Happy Birthday", let alone give Katrina the card and present she'd promised. It was weird.

When the teacher walked in with the register, Katrina had another surprise. Their usual Mr Wilson had been replaced by a supply teacher. She was amazingly tall and startlingly beautiful – like a supermodel, or a film star: the kind of person you expect to see climbing out of a limousine, wearing a long dress and dripping in diamonds. She was far too gorgeous to be walking around a school. The whole class let out gasps of astonishment when she walked in.

"Good morning," said the teacher, her eyes running hungrily over every child in the class as if she were devouring their faces. "My name is Miss Fay." Her gaze rested on Katrina and for a moment they stared at each other. A prickle of terror ran down Katrina's spine. For that brief moment she could feel that – beautiful as Miss Fay was – there was something cold and terrifying about her: her heart was solid ice.

Miss Fay opened the register, breaking off eye contact with Katrina, and began to call out names.

Katrina blinked several times and gave herself a shake, trying to throw off the sensation of dread that clutched at her. She must be imagining things. But maybe she ought to get Mum to take her to the opticians and have her eyes tested, because when she looked at Miss Fay again she seemed to be shrouded in a very faint haze of red mist.

Katrina's class were going on a trip to the Clifton Suspension Bridge that day. They were doing a project on the Victorians with Mr Wilson and the bridge was a famous feat of Victorian engineering by a man called Isambard Kingdom Brunel.

Katrina had been pleased that the outing coincided with her birthday, and Mum had even given her a special packed lunch for the occasion, with her favourite crisps and a chocolate bar. But now she had a hollow feeling in the bottom of her stomach which refused to move. It gnawed and nagged at her, and grew into a stab of dreadful panic every time Miss Fay looked her way. Something odd was going on, Katrina was sure of it. But she didn't know what it was, and she had absolutely no idea what to do about it.

From the minute they trooped into the lobby to wait for the coach, Katrina's day went from bad to really dreadful. Daisy stood in a huddle with the other girls in their class. She hadn't said a word to Katrina since the start of school and now they all turned their backs every time Katrina came close.

When the coach pulled up, the girls sat in their usual pairs and Katrina thought that she and Daisy were bound to sit together – they always did. But Daisy chose a place beside Jordan Smith, a nasty little bully who was always picking on the Year One kids. Only a really big fall out could have induced Katrina's best friend to sit with him. Katrina didn't know what she had done to deserve it – it wasn't like they'd had an argument or anything. She was confused and hurt. The only place left for her was at the front next to Miss Fay.

The weird thing was, Miss Fay seemed pleased. Every now and then her eyes flicked across to

Katrina, and she would give a little smile – just a faint curl of her lips that Katrina could see out of the corner of her eye. And sometimes she seemed to be sniffing slightly like a large animal smelling out its prey. Miss Fay was scenting the air like a hungry tiger.

Katrina also had the peculiar sensation that the air between herself and Miss Fay was almost solid. It made her think of the fridge magnets at home – they'd cling happily to the fridge, but if she took two off and tried to put them together it was impossible – they'd slide away from each other as if pushed apart by an invisible force. Katrina felt like a fridge magnet as she sat – squashed hard against the coach window – as though held there by an unseen hand.

It was only a few miles to the bridge but what with the morning rush hour and the roadworks, the journey lasted nearly an hour. It was the longest hour of Katrina's life. She sat in silence. In fact they all sat in silence. It was very strange. The class should have been chattering with excitement and singing silly songs and eating their packed lunches. But no one spoke. There wasn't a murmur as they moved slowly through the heavy traffic and the pouring rain.

Eventually the coach pulled up on the Downs, a large area of flat, open grassland near the bridge. Miss Fay led the class – who obediently trooped along behind her towards the Avon gorge. As they reached the edge, the ground simply dropped away. It was like standing on top of a cliff, only there was a river at the bottom, not sea. It was as if a giant hand had sliced the earth in two with a blunt knife.

Perched perilously on either side of the chasm were two towers, which held the thick cables that the bridge was suspended from.

The wind whistled, and the rain lashed down in great sheets. It suited Katrina's mood, which had gone from the rosy pink anticipation of a lovely birthday, to cold, black depression.

Katrina knew the bridge well. She saw it in the distance every time she went to the supermarket with her parents, but she had never actually walked across it.

Katrina didn't like heights at the best of times, and on a day like today the bridge looked distinctly flimsy – as if there was nothing but a wafer thin set of planks between the traffic and a very long drop.

Miss Fay threw Katrina a look that made her stomach lurch, and then, without saying a word, led the way across the pedestrian walkway at the side of the bridge. The class followed silently in single file, but Katrina hung around at the back so that she could stay on solid land for as long as possible. All too soon everyone was on the bridge and Katrina had no choice but to follow.

Katrina stepped on to the walkway and looked down. It was horrible. The river snaked through the gorge below. It was low tide and there were expanses of brown river mud to suck you in and drag you under.

"Look at the horizon," she told herself, forcing her gaze up. She could just about see the hills in the distance. She took a deep breath, but the drop pulled her vision like a magnet, and soon she was peering into the abyss again, feeling dizzy and light-headed as if she might topple in at any moment. "Stop it," she told herself firmly, "Come on, Katrina, get a grip." Jaws clenched with determination, she lifted her head and fixed her eyes on the landscape beyond. Taking another deep breath, she swallowed hard and tried to steady herself.

Suddenly, everything stopped.

The wind didn't just drop – it ceased completely. The gust that had been tugging at Katrina's hair froze in a cold, solid lump by her ear. The rain halted, drops hanging in mid-air. Drivers paused motionless behind the wheels of their cars; a cyclist balanced precariously on two wheels; and a plane that had been passing overhead was frozen, unmoving, a thousand feet above them.

Katrina's class was spread out along the footpath as still as a photograph. Daisy had tripped, and was teetering at a perilous angle, about to fall but unable to do so.

The silence was absolute.

Katrina had seen something like it in the summer holidays when Merlin had frozen Mum and her brother Adrian. But this wasn't just two people – it seemed to be the whole of Bristol.

It was then that Katrina understood with perfect clarity that the necklace hadn't been an accident.

There was magic at work.

Bad magic.

An icy voice cut through the silence, making Katrina's blood run cold.

"Katrina Picket." It was Miss Fay. Standing at the end of the footpath. Not frozen. She looked at Katrina with piercing eyes. "Katrina Picket, I will not tolerate a rival. You must cease."

Miss Fay stretched out her arms, pointed her fingers at Katrina and muttered something inaudible.

A blast of red hot sparks slammed into Katrina's chest. There was a piercing sensation and Katrina felt something shatter deep inside her. Before she realized what was happening, she was thrown upwards and over the barrier. She was hovering above the gorge.

It had been bad enough looking at the drop from the safety of the bridge. Hanging in mid-air it was terrifying.

"Cease *what*?" squeaked Katrina, looking over her shoulder at Miss Fay. "What have I *done*?"

Miss Fay said nothing. She smiled – a cold, humourless sneer. Then she let Katrina fall.

Katrina kicked against the frozen air and flung herself with all her might at the bridge.

She missed.

But she did manage to catch on to the work-men's iron cage that hung underneath. She clung to it with one hand.

Help! she thought desperately. *Oh help ... help ... someone ... please... HELP!*

There was a flash, a crash, and a very loud *pop*! The smell of burnt-out fireworks exploded and suddenly there, standing on the pedestrian walk-way above Katrina, was Merlin.

Merlin? *Merlin? Merlin!*

Merlin – who was supposed to be in America! Merlin – who, in fact, had been in Disneyland until that very moment. He looked around him in sur-prise, saw Katrina hanging below him, and guiltily hid the silver wand he had been brandishing behind his back.

Then he noticed Miss Fay.

All the colour drained from Merlin's face.

Miss Fay glared furiously back at Merlin. Then she disappeared in a shower of red sparks.

"Oh dear," said Merlin breathlessly. He sat down hard on the walkway. "Dear, dear, dear. What an unpleasant surprise. Oh my goodness."

"Er, Merlin," called Katrina from beneath the bridge. She was delighted to see him, but she needed some help; she was still dangling over the gorge.

"What?" he said, irritably.

"Can you help?" she asked. "Please?"

"Oh for heaven's sake, let go!" he snapped.

"What?"

"Katrinapicket," he said sternly. "Do you remember nothing from the summer?"

"Er…" said Katrina. Her fingers were slipping.

"You are a sorceress," he said.

"Help!" she pleaded.

"Let go," he said.

I'm going to die, she thought. *I can't believe it. He's going to let me die. It's my birthday.* She sniffed to herself. Then her fingers gave up. She fell.

But Katrina Picket was indeed a sorceress.

She didn't fall down.

She fell up.

Up and over the barrier, landing gently on the bridge next to Merlin.

"*There* you are," he said irritably. "You took your time."

He was looking worried, Katrina realized with

shock. She had never seen him look quite like that.

"Where's Miss Fay?" she asked.

"Gone," he replied. "Took herself off. For the moment."

"What's that?" she said, looking at the silver wand. Merlin blushed and coughed and muttered something that sounded like "stage prop". Then he threw it into the dustbin at the side of the path.

"Bit of rubbish I picked up on my travels," he said. "Souvenir thing. Don't need it now. Anyway, better get on and unfreeze everyone, I suppose. Typical of her to just disappear. She'd leave the whole of Bristol to rot. The entire kingdom could perish for all she cares."

Purple sparks flew from his fingertips and before Katrina could open her mouth to say anything, time had started again, and Merlin had gone.

Katrina looked with astonishment at the end of the bridge. Standing exactly where Miss Fay had been, talking calmly about Brunel's engineering skill, was Mr Wilson, their class teacher.

Miss Who?

It was as if Miss Fay had never existed. As if that morning had simply not happened.

Time started. Daisy tripped, recovered, and looked around for her best friend, Katrina.

"What are you doing back there?" she asked coming towards her. She looked closely at Katrina, taking in the pale face and wide eyes.

"Are you OK, Kat?" she asked. "You don't like heights, do you? Do you want me to get Mr Wilson?"

"Where's Miss Fay?" asked Katrina.

"Who?" Daisy was puzzled.

"You know – Miss Fay. The supply teacher."

Daisy looked blank. "What supply teacher?" she said. "What are you on about?"

"Who did you sit next to on the way here?" Katrina asked.

"You, of course. Who else would I sit next to? Jordan Smith?" Daisy laughed. "Kat, you look a bit sick. I'm going to get Mr Wilson."

They put it down to a bad attack of vertigo. They thought her fear of heights had made her light headed and a bit dizzy.

"Nothing to worry about," said Mr Wilson kindly. But at the end of the day he gave her a note to take home to Mum, "Just in case."

Daisy came home with Katrina after school and they had birthday tea with all the trimmings – sausages on sticks, cheese and pineapple cubes, egg and cress sandwiches with the crusts cut off, crisps, chocolate fingers and fairy cakes. Katrina was getting a bit old for this kind of tea, but it was the only party food that Mum and Dad would ever make: they always gave the same to Adrian when he had a birthday and he was already grown up. Katrina had to force herself to eat: the sausages tasted like polystyrene, and the cheese and pineapple stuck in her throat. She forced herself to smile when Adrian brought her cake through; the eleven flaming candles brought the thought of poor Bernard, lying in ashes in her drawer, to the front of her mind. It took all Katrina's willpower to draw enough breath to blow them out. By the time they got to the cinema, Katrina's face was aching with all the forced smiling. When the lights dimmed and the adverts started, Katrina sighed with relief. At last she didn't have to talk to anyone. She could sit in the dark and think.

After school the next day, Daisy had a dental appointment, and was whisked away speedily by her mum. Katrina was relieved. Daisy had been throwing her anxious glances all day. Katrina knew she hadn't been herself. It was hard to relax with so many worrying thoughts buzzing around in her head. So she was utterly delighted to see Merlin waiting for her outside the school gates.

They walked down the hill towards Victoria Park and sat on a bench near the playground.

"Miss Fay was there but no one remembers," said Katrina. "It's really spooky. And Daisy's suddenly my best friend again – she didn't speak to me yesterday morning and now she's fine. Did Miss Fay make her do it?"

Merlin sucked his teeth thoughtfully. "It was always her way," he said. "Mind games, trickery, playing with people's emotions. Little hobby of hers, really. Cunning and devious, she is. Nasty piece of work. Sorry to see her back."

Katrina swallowed nervously. "So," she said, "she's not really a supply teacher, then?"

Merlin shook his head, "Alas, no, she is not."

"Well who is she?" said Katrina, baffled. "Who is she really?"

Merlin looked at Katrina and sighed wearily. "She is the most powerful sorceress that ever lived. She is Morgan le Fay."

The name rang a bell in Katrina's head. During the summer holidays – before she'd banished

Merlin from the house – Mum had told her all about King Arthur and the Round Table. She remembered Mum's description of Morgan le Fay. "King Arthur's half-sister. A real baddie."

"Hang on a minute," said Katrina. "When we were talking to Mum that time, she asked you where Morgan was now, and you said—"

"Everywhere and Nowhere," said Merlin. "She is the evil that dwells in men's hearts … yes, indeed. It was true. It still is. She infects minds and hearts; she thrives on discord; she spreads wickedness as a foul, contagious disease. But until yesterday she had existed as a *general* evil. Now it seems she has found something to inspire a very *particular* hatred. It has caused her to take a body again. To manifest herself in human form." He looked at Katrina sadly and said, "Katrinapicket, I am very much afraid that she has focussed on you."

Katrina gulped. "Why?" It came out as a small, breathless whisper. "What have I done?"

Merlin placed a hand on her shoulder. "Katrinapicket, you have done a great deal to earn her enmity. You woke me from my slumbers. That alone will have upset her. But you also saved the kingdom." Merlin looked at Katrina, his eyes weary and anxious. "Did she speak to you?"

"Yes," said Katrina, recalling the words Miss Fay had flung at her before the red sparks slammed into her chest. "She said she wouldn't tolerate a rival. She said I must cease. But cease what? I haven't been doing anything. Not to her. Have I?"

Merlin smiled sadly. "I'm afraid you have, simply by existing. It is as I feared: she has felt your power, she knows its strength. She wants to destroy you before you are trained because afterwards she thinks you'll be more than a match for her. It's quite a compliment, really."

Katrina could think of several other ways she'd rather be complimented than by Morgan trying to kill her. And she still didn't understand why Morgan thought they were in some sort of competition in the first place. "I don't *want* to fight with her," she said, almost to herself.

"I'm very much afraid that you don't have any choice in the matter," declared Merlin. "Now she has found you, she won't let the matter rest. You are a force for good, you see, and she can't stand that. Goodness, honesty, they repel her, sicken her.

She'll do anything she can to rid the world of them. And you."

A little squeaking noise escaped from Katrina's throat, but she said nothing. Merlin stared at the trees in the park, frowning, and plucking at his beard.

Eventually, Katrina said, "So when she whooshed me over the bridge, would I have fallen down, or up?"

"Down, undoubtedly," answered Merlin. "Remember the first time you fell up? In the cave when you found me?"

Katrina nodded. How could she forget clinging to the roof of the cave like an iron filing on a magnet?

"Magic attracts magic. That's why you were drawn to the cave roof. With Morgan things are different. Evil magic repels good. And she was blocking your powers just to be on the safe side. No, if you hadn't summoned me, you'd be dead by now. But she obviously didn't know the full extent of your strength. Not then, anyway. She certainly didn't expect me to appear."

That makes two of us, thought Katrina. She wasn't at all sure how she'd managed to summon Merlin, but she was very glad she had. Her mind flitted back to the package with the smoky "M" that rose from it. "That necklace must have been from her," she said.

"Necklace? What necklace?"

Katrina described it, and what it had done to poor, unfortunate Bernard.

"That old trick," Merlin said, shaking his head crossly. "She tried much the same thing on Arthur once. Sent him a cloak as a gift. Arthur wasn't fooled, though. He put the cloak on the messenger who had brought it. It wasn't pretty. Messenger was reduced to ashes in a moment. Nasty."

"Why does she hate Arthur so much?" asked Katrina. It felt sort of comforting to know that Morgan hated someone besides herself.

"She's his *sister*," said Merlin. "Jealous from the moment he was born. And she didn't grow out of it like normal people do. She fed and nurtured it, and encouraged the hatred to grow. I dare say *she* thinks she has reason enough. But really Morgan hates Arthur *because* she hates him. It is her nature to hate, as it is Arthur's nature to love." There was a slight pause before Merlin added quietly, "You must keep your wits about you, Katrinapicket. You're going to need them."

I could be dead, thought Katrina. *Instant bonfire, or flat as a pancake. I wonder what she'll do next?*

"Well," said Merlin decisively. "If Morgan is active again there are some things that need to be done. Who knows what she will do, now she's back? When her temper is aroused she is utterly deadly. If she gets herself into a passion for destruction then nothing and no one will be safe. Last time she destroyed the entire kingdom just to get at Arthur. I must warn him, for a start. And Lancelot and Guinevere. She spoiled things for them last time. Used Mordred to wreck the Round Table. He was her creature, you see? No doubt she'll try something similar again." Merlin looked Katrina in the eyes. "Katrinapicket, we must start your training right away."

It was going to be difficult to arrange. Katrina had school and homework to fit in, and they had to keep it all secret from Mum and Dad. Dad would probably just go into the garden shed and refuse to come out as usual. But if Mum knew Merlin was back she'd be on to the police instantly and that could cause all sorts of terrible complications.

"Couldn't you freeze them?" asked Katrina.

"The whole of Bristol?" said Merlin.

"No – just Mum and Dad. Then we could train at home."

"I think not, Katrinapicket. They would lose too much time. They would notice. They would begin to suspect. Or they would think they were going mad. No, we must find another way. Let us concentrate, and see what we can do."

In the end, the solution they came up with was Daisy.

"You're a *what*?" Daisy's eyes were wide.

Katrina had arrived at her house and said there was something she needed to talk about.

"I'm a sorceress."

"A sorceress?" Daisy dissolved in fits of giggles. "Go on then, prove it."

Katrina did.

First she tried a couple of blasts from her fingertips – she'd managed to transform rocks into snapdragons that way once – but absolutely nothing happened. She hadn't been trained yet, that was the problem: she couldn't make things happen just because she wanted them to.

So Katrina performed the only bit of magic she knew.

She went out of Daisy's bedroom and on to the landing. Checking that no one but Daisy was watching, Katrina climbed on to the banister rail, stretched her arms wide, and dived off, head first. She plummeted down and grazed her nose on the carpet of the bottom stair, then, like a bungee jumper on a rope, she sprang back up and landed softly on the landing.

Daisy stood open mouthed. "Do that again," she said.

"No!" said Katrina, rubbing her nose. It was sore.

"How did you do that?"

"I told you – I'm a sorceress."

"Can you teach me?"

"No!" exclaimed Katrina. The conversation was going in completely the wrong direction. "Look, Daisy, I don't know how it works. I didn't even know I had powers until the summer holidays."

"How did you find out? Do you think I could get them too?"

"No," said Katrina. "Look, you can't go into a shop and buy them. It just sort of happened." She sat down on Daisy's bed and told her about the events of the summer. "And now Morgan's after me, and Merlin wants to train me properly," she concluded. "But I can't tell Mum and Dad what I'm doing."

Daisy's eyes gleamed with excitement. She didn't seem to be taking the threat to Katrina's life very seriously. Still, at least she was prepared to help.

"OK," said Daisy eagerly. "What do I do?"

It was arranged: Merlin would train Katrina after school; Katrina would tell Mum and Dad that she was spending the time at Daisy's working on a school project. All Daisy needed to do was cover for her.

A simple plan. And, like all simple plans, so much could go wrong.

The Royal Stilton

The big problem was where Merlin should stay. Last time, he had slept in the spare room at Katrina's house. There was no way he could do that now. Where could you put an elderly sorcerer in a velvet dress who was fond of toast and marmalade? He couldn't just sleep on a park bench. Could he?

"Absolutely not," said Merlin firmly. "I had quite enough of that on my travels with Desmond. No Katrinapicket, I think the time has come for me to experience a little luxury. Where is the best hostelry?"

An eventful bus ride followed. Merlin had problems with his dress. It was a new one, Katrina noticed, much more voluminous than his old one. In fact, there was so much of it, that it caught in the bus door and short-circuited the mechanism. The bus driver had to call out an engineer from the depot to release him.

At last, Merlin and Katrina arrived at Cathedral Green, home of the Royal Stilton Hotel: five stars, elegant, impressive, very luxurious and very expensive.

Merlin reversed off the bus with difficulty.

"Farewell, Sir Busdriver!" he waved cheerfully. The doors shut with a hiss, narrowly missing Merlin's beard. The driver stamped on the accelerator with more force than was strictly necessary and the bus shot forward, sending passengers thumping back against their seats and causing a few stiff necks.

"Oh yes!" said Merlin looking around. "This will do nicely. Let us proceed forthwith."

Merlin marched confidently across the green, up the steps and into the very grand lobby. Katrina trailed along behind, feeling like any eleven year old in school uniform – out of place and uncomfortable.

"Now then," said Merlin. "Where shall I begin? Room at the top, I think." He set off for the staircase.

A huge security guard in smart uniform appeared from nowhere, blocking Merlin's path.

Merlin stepped to the left.

So did the guard.

Merlin stepped to the right.

So did the guard.

Merlin looked at the guard.

The guard looked at Merlin and smiled. It was not a welcoming smile. He cracked his knuckles.

"Can I help, sir?" came the silky voice of the hotel receptionist. She had come out from behind her desk and crossed the lobby, sensing trouble. She threw the security guard a warning look. For all they knew, Merlin was an eccentric millionaire. It didn't do to beat up potential customers.

"I need somewhere to stay," explained Merlin huffily. "I thought this would do. I was just off to find a room but this silly man got in the way."

"Could you step this way please, sir?" The receptionist gently guided Merlin towards her desk. Her elaborate display of courtesy pleased him no end.

"I'm not a *sir*," he said patiently. "I'm not a *knight*, you see? I'm a *sorcerer*. Merlin's the name."

"Well, Mr Merlin," said the receptionist, beaming brightly. "Let's see what we can do." She glided behind her desk and said smoothly, "A single room, Mr Merlin? Or would you like a suite?"

"A sweet?" Merlin looked puzzled. "No thank you. Not hungry."

Katrina stepped in. "Not a *sweet*," she said. "A *suite* – it's when you have more than one room, I think." She looked at the receptionist who nodded and continued to smile unwaveringly.

"How strange," said Merlin. "Well, let me see. I shall be here for some time. And we'll need a lot of space for the training. A suite, I think. Biggest one you've got."

"That would be the penthouse," said the receptionist. She gave a discreet little cough and then said in delicate tones, "And how will you be paying, Mr Merlin?"

"Paying?" said Merlin loudly.

The receptionist blushed. "Yes, sir. Do you have a credit card...?"

The question hung in the air.

The security guard hovered menacingly.

Katrina pulled Merlin aside. "Merlin, we need to pay for this." She cursed herself for her stupidity. If her mind hadn't been so full of Morgan le Fay's murder attempts she would have thought about it before.

"Pay?" said Merlin, utterly mystified. "What do you mean?"

"*Pay!*" said Katrina. She didn't know how to make it clearer. "With *money*."

"Money?" said Merlin. "*Money?*" he repeated and laughed. "I've got *piles* of the stuff. *Wondered* what it was for."

Katrina watched in astonishment as – from the sleeve of his velvet dress – Merlin ejected a fountain of cash. Thousands and thousands of notes and coins cascaded over the reception desk.

"Er, I think that will do, Merlin," said Katrina, as the desk cracked under the weight and Merlin's money fountain still showed no signs of letting up. "You can save the rest for later."

"Very well," said Merlin.

The receptionist straightened her glasses and looked at the security guard in triumph. He cracked his knuckles in disappointment and went back to skulk in his office under the stairs.

"Wayne will take you up to the penthouse, Mr Merlin," she said, calling a porter. "I'll just get all this counted and put in the safe. Would that suit you, sir?"

Merlin waved his hand airily. "Do what you like with it," he said carelessly. "Filthy stuff," he said to Katrina on the way to the lift.

The penthouse was at the top of the hotel. Wayne threw open the door. It was splendid.

"Good heavens," said Merlin. "You exchange all those silly bits of paper and metal for this? Nearly threw it all away last week, it was getting so heavy. Just as well I didn't, eh? My, oh my. This beats the spare room."

He looked into the bathroom. "Do a lot of

gnomes visit Bristol?" he asked, pointing at the bidet. "They've put in a bath for them, look."

"Yes," said Katrina nodding her head. "There are an awful lot of gnomes here." She wasn't going to explain the bidet. It had been embarrassing enough showing Merlin how the toilet in her house worked during the summer.

Katrina changed the subject. "Where did all your money come from?" she asked.

"People kept giving it to me," said Merlin. "Everywhere we went, Desmond and I. Everything we did. Very strange. We'd be sitting there, minding our own business, having a game of chess in the park. I'd get the board out of its box, set up the pieces and put the empty box down next to me. The next thing I knew people were dropping money into it. Couldn't stop them. Thought it was some strange new custom."

Katrina imagined the scene. People must have thought they were street entertainers – very impressive buskers. No wonder they had made a small fortune.

"Then this chap with a funny accent came up to us, wanting us to go to Disneyland. He transported us to America on a flying machine, Katrinapicket! It was quite astonishing. Between you and me, I must confess that it was a lot more comfortable than a dragon – not so windy, you see? Desmond had to flap along behind, of course, he wouldn't fit inside. And once we were there we were allowed to eat as many hamburgers as we liked – that's a lot in Desmond's case – as long as we promised to march up and down a bit. It was all quite nice really."

"So that's where the silver wand came from."

Merlin blushed and scratched his ear. "Yes, well, they liked it. Added authenticity, they said, whatever that means. Got me new robes too. And a hat. It must have fallen off when you summoned me. We were in the middle of a parade – gosh!" he said suddenly. "I must write to Desmond at once! He'll be wondering what on earth's happened to me. And Arthur too. He and Lancelot and Guinevere have a nice little apartment in San Francisco. I'm afraid the news of Morgan's return is going to upset them terribly. Do you have a quill?"

Katrina didn't. Merlin couldn't seem to manage a biro, so Katrina wrote his letters for him on the hotel notepaper.

Dear Desmond,

Sorry I left so suddenly. Sir Katrinapicket summoned me. She was in mortal peril. Morgan le Fay is back.

See you when I can.

Love Merlin.

PS Knight to E4.

"What does that mean?" asked Katrina.

"Chess game. That's my next move," answered Merlin. "I'm winning."

Then Katrina added her own PS:

Thanks for the birthday present. It's beautiful. Missing you. K.

To Arthur, they wrote:

Dear Arthur, Guinevere and Lancelot,

Have returned to Albion to assist Sir Katrinapicket. Morgan is back. Be careful.

Love Merlin.

Katrina couldn't think of anything to write, so she put some kisses on the bottom.

"Now," said Merlin. "Let us get these despatched forthwith."

They made their way back to the reception desk.

"Now, my lady," said Merlin. "Terribly sorry, I don't believe I know your name."

"I'm Pat," she said, smiling brightly. "Pat Bennett."

"Good heavens! What a very strange name," said Merlin. "Well, Lady Patpatbennett, where are your pigeons?"

"I *beg* your pardon?" Pat Bennett was so startled that her smile slipped. Eccentric was one thing, but *mad* was quite another.

"Your pigeons," said Merlin. "Better make sure they are sturdy ones, they have a very long journey to make."

Katrina intervened before Pat Bennett could call the security guard. "We need to send two letters to America."

"Oh, I see." Pat Bennett fetched stamps and Katrina stuck them on. Merlin watched in amazement.

"And *these* have replaced pigeons ... goodness me! Will they really transport these letters? They don't look strong enough." He examined the stamps closely as if he expected them to sprout wings.

"They'll get there," said Katrina, smiling sweetly at Pat Bennett. "Trust me."

As soon as the door of the penthouse suite closed behind them, Merlin shot purple sparks at Katrina. She flew across the room and hit the opposite wall.

"Ow!" she said indignantly.

"Ha!" said Merlin. "Took you by surprise. You need to be more alert, Katrinapicket. It's time to start teaching you Major Magic."

Training

Every day after school, Katrina waved a winking, conspiratorial Daisy goodbye and caught the bus to the Royal Stilton for her training sessions.

Morgan hadn't tried anything since Merlin's arrival, but Katrina could feel her dark presence batting against her consciousness: she was out there, biding her time, watching and waiting for the chance to make her move. And with two failed murder attempts behind her, Morgan's mood would be deadlier than ever. Katrina wondered what she would dream up next. It was nerve-wracking, but at least the training kept her mind occupied; there was an awful lot to learn.

"Strictly speaking," Merlin had told her, "we shouldn't begin until after your twelfth birthday – that's the age of Magical Responsibility, you see? But given the circumstances, I think we can bend the rules a bit. And then of course, we'd usually start with a little quest to prove your suitability. But really, the events of the summer have shown you to be more than capable."

Merlin began Katrina's training with self-defence. "First things first," he said decisively. "Our priority must be to keep you alive. Everything else can come later."

Katrina was expecting Merlin to teach her some spells – she'd thought there might be words to learn like the invocation with which she'd raised Avalon in the summer. But it wasn't that easy.

"There are an infinite number of ways Morgan could attack you, Katrinapicket. I cannot teach you sufficient defensive charms to deal with them all – there simply isn't the time. And the last thing you want to be doing is trying to remember the words to a particular charm in the heat of battle. No. *You* must learn to protect *yourself*," he urged her. "Sadly, I cannot tell you precisely how. There is no recipe, no secret formula. You must find your own core of inner strength. Your own magical source. It's rather like a deep pool of water. Draw on it. Wrap yourself in it. Use it as a shield to deflect whatever is hurled at you."

Merlin cracked his knuckles. It seemed the only way to teach Katrina self-defence was by attacking her. "Let's see what you can do," said Merlin enthusiastically. "I'll begin my assault with elementals."

Elementals turned out to be rather frightening. Merlin conjured up each of the four elements in turn – earth, air, fire, water – and threw them at her. Katrina couldn't imagine how the hotel cleaners were going to feel about it as she and the thick white carpet were showered with mud and doused with water.

For the first few sessions Merlin simply sat on the bed and attacked Katrina from across the room. He hurled small tornadoes at her while she shivered in a corner. He surrounded her with a circle of burning

flames. He soaked her with a deluge of rain and froze her in a block of ice. Try as she might, Katrina couldn't do a thing to protect herself. It was all very bruising. She staggered home each afternoon feeling as if she had run several marathons. The worst of it was that Katrina knew Merlin was being kind: she was well aware that he hadn't unleashed anything like his full force at her. If it was this hard when *Merlin* was doing these things, how much worse would it be when Morgan got hold of her? And it did seem to be a question of *when* and not *if* – Merlin didn't seem to be in any doubt that Katrina would have to face Morgan eventually. And however much he smiled at her with encouragement, she could still see the anxiety in his eyes.

And then, after a scorching session in which Merlin had singed nearly every piece of furniture in the penthouse suite, Merlin had a vision.

He had been sitting on the slightly charred bed when he had suddenly fallen backwards and his eyes had rolled up into his head. Katrina wasn't especially alarmed – she'd seen Merlin examining his inner eye once before – so she simply waited for him to come to. It didn't last long, but when Merlin sat up he was white and his hands were trembling. The content of his vision had shaken him to the core.

"Devastation … annihilation… The kingdom laid to waste… Dead, Katrinapicket … all dead…"

"Who?" whispered Katrina, dreading his answer.

"Everyone," Merlin's voice cracked with pain. "Arthur, Lancelot, Guinevere." Merlin looked at Katrina with terrified eyes. "All of them."

Katrina forced herself to think. "They're not here," she said firmly. "They're safe in America. That can't have been a vision of what's going to happen. Maybe you just saw what happened last time: the battle that finished the Round Table. That could be it, couldn't it?"

"Possibly," he said, his voice trembling a little. "Yes, maybe you are right, Katrinapicket. Perhaps I saw the past, and not the future." But as he said it, he avoided her eyes.

Anxiety clouded everything Katrina did. For the first two weeks, she made no progress whatsoever with her training. Merlin could tell her to look for her inner strength until he was blue in the face, but she just couldn't find it. The harder she tried, the more it seemed to slip from her grasp, like sand through her fingers.

Then one afternoon – while Merlin sat on the bed casually blasting a howling gale at her with one finger – Katrina had a breakthrough. The wind was whistling past her ears and sucking her breath away, exactly as it had done when she'd been riding on Desmond's back in the summer, hurtling down towards London in pursuit of a fireball. The thought of Desmond exploded like a bomb of happiness in her mind: she recalled precisely how she'd felt when she'd transformed the burning rocks into snapdragons. And then she found it: her core of inner strength; the still source of magic at her centre; the deep, calm pool. Quietly – holding her breath in case she lost the sense of it again – she dipped her mind into it like a bucket into a well. Katrina drew it up, wrapped herself with the feeling of power and *BANG!* She deflected the howling gale back at Merlin so efficiently that he was thrown clean off the bed.

"Oh well done!" he shouted enthusiastically,

picking himself up and shaking the wastepaper bin off his foot. "Marvellous! We have progress! Real progress at last!" He surveyed the hole Katrina's blast had made in the wall. "Mmmm," he murmured. "And perhaps now's the time to teach you a little Restoration."

Restoration was reasonably straightforward. Without the pressure of being under attack, Katrina found it fairly easy to focus her mind and draw up sufficient magic to sprinkle the wall with the pink sparks that obediently flew from her fingertips. A single word of command – "Restore!" – the smell of burnt-out fireworks – and lumps of plaster leapt back into position until no more than a hairline crack showed in the paint work.

Once Katrina had mastered deflecting elementals, Merlin decided it was time to start attacking her in different ways. The following afternoon he moved on to Involuntary Transformations – showering her in purple sparks and turning her into a cat, a rat, and then a mouse. Every time Katrina's body exploded into a million fragments and reassembled itself into something smaller, it made her feel dizzy and slightly sick. Merlin was changing her so quickly that she didn't have time to focus – she couldn't adjust to where her inner core was in a different body. Katrina was getting hot and flustered and grumpy, and then – the final indignity – Merlin changed her into a worm. Katrina didn't like that at all.

Room service arrived as she lay there, wriggling helplessly on the floor, squashed so uncomfortably in the teeny tiny body that she couldn't find her inner core at all, let alone make use of it. The waiter – who was carrying a tray of tea and toast and marmalade – nearly trod on her. When he spotted her, he picked her up and said with some distaste, "Shall I remove the worm, sir?"

"No, no, no," said Merlin irritably. "Put her down at once. She's in training."

The waiter laid Katrina gently back on the carpet. "Very good, sir," he said smoothly, and went out. He hadn't so much as raised an eyebrow. The hotel staff all knew that Merlin was an eccentric millionaire. He had filled the walk-in shower cubicle full of cash – shooting it from the sleeve of his dress on his first night with evident relief. The staff would indulge any eccentricities just as long as he paid his bill.

Katrina lay wriggling crossly on the floor. She couldn't do anything! And then she realized that her anger was getting in the way. She wouldn't be able to change back unless she calmed down. She took a small, wormy breath and very deliberately stretched out long and still on the grubby white carpet. She reached as deeply as she could into her little slimy body until – *pop!* – she was herself again.

"Very good!" said Merlin happily. "My, my, you are doing well! Let's have some tea now, shall we?"

They had tea and toast. Merlin had ordered every type of marmalade on the menu, and fifteen little pots were lined up side by side on the tray. It had been a revelation to him when he discovered that you could get different sorts.

"Look!" he exclaimed as he examined a pot of lime marmalade. "A green one! Good heavens!" He tasted it. "Inestimably magnificent," he declared, and lapsed into happy silence while he chewed.

Katrina was silent too. She was trying to absorb what she'd learnt. Merlin had got swifter in his assaults, changing her before she had time to deflect his blasts. And this was just the beginning. Clearly it wasn't enough to find her inner core and use it once she was under attack – by then it might be too late. Katrina had to find a way of holding her defensive shield in her mind all the time. But it seemed to take such a lot of concentration, and she couldn't do anything else at the same time – like walk or talk. Maybe it was something she would be able to manage once she'd had enough practice, like patting her head and rubbing her tummy. Perhaps it was just a matter of co-ordination. But would that be any use even if she did master it? Morgan had blocked her powers before, hadn't she? How had she done that?

"How do you block someone's powers?" asked Katrina. "Could I do it to Morgan?"

"No," said Merlin, flatly. "Power blocking involves seeking out someone else's inner core and shattering it. You've barely found your own: on absolutely no account must you search for Morgan's. Hers is so dark, so deadly, such utter poison that I doubt that you would survive a brush against it."

Katrina remembered the cold, icy wave that had pierced her when she'd been thrown over the bridge. The sensation of something shattering deep inside. She'd thought it had been her own terror, but now knew it must have been Morgan blocking her. And yet somehow she'd summoned Merlin.

"I don't understand," Katrina said.

"Mmmmm?" said Merlin distantly. He had discovered a pot of three fruits marmalade.

"Morgan," she said. "If she blocked my powers, how did I summon you?"

"Ah," said Merlin, thoughtfully. "Interesting point Katrinapicket." There was a pause while Merlin turned it over in his mind. When he spoke next, Katrina thought she could see a tiny glimmer of hope flickering in his eyes. "Your powers at present are unequal and Morgan is so very, very strong. If you'd tried to fight back she'd have blasted you to bits with no trouble at all. But you didn't, you went around her." Merlin was silent for a few moments. "I think you may have something there Katrinapicket. Perhaps you have found the key. You must devise a route *around* anything she throws at you. Do what she doesn't expect. That's the way forward."

"But what will she try next?" Katrina wondered aloud.

"Who can tell?" said Merlin. "She's crafty, devious and destructive. One thing's certain, though: we need to get as much training in as we can. You need as many skills at your disposal as possible. Because whatever she does next, you won't be expecting it. All you can do is keep your wits about you and react when it comes. Don't waste time worrying about it before it gets here."

They finished the toast. Merlin lined up the pots of marmalade on the mantelpiece. It was quite a collection. Then it was time to leave. Katrina – tired, but enormously satisfied that she was at last getting somewhere with her training – went home.

Restoring Bernard

Katrina caught the bus back. She called "hello" to Dad, who was drinking tea in the kitchen, then went upstairs to do her homework. Before she started, she looked in her drawer.

"I wonder," she murmured. "I wonder…"

If she could restore plaster, perhaps she could restore a bear, too.

She pulled out the bag of ashes and placed it on top of her chest of drawers, right on the scorch mark where Bernard had been sitting before he'd been incinerated.

Katrina focussed her mind, found her inner core and drew it up. She concentrated hard, until her mental energy felt needle sharp, held out her hands and pointed her fingers at Bernard.

"Restore," she said softly.

Nothing much happened. The bag rustled faintly, but that was all. Katrina tutted impatiently, emptied the ashes out in a powdery grey cloud and tried again.

"Restore," she said. "Come on, Bernard, please."

Pink sparks flew from her fingertips and shot across the room.

Ashy powder became ashy flakes. Ashy flakes became ashy lumps. Ashy lumps became charred dollops of stuffing, and fragments of blackened fur. The dollops and fragments of Bernard lay for a moment on the chest of drawers like a strange jig-saw puzzle, then started pulling themselves together. Like a film running backwards, Katrina's teddy was restored.

"Bernard!" she said, with delight. She was quite pleased to see him, but she was absolutely *thrilled* she had done some magic all on her own, without

Merlin instructing her what to do! She gave her teddy a triumphant squeeze, kissed him on his bald patch and did a little dance on the spot, hugging him to her chest. He was a bit scorched in places, and he smelt funny, but he was back. "I did it! I did it!"

Katrina's triumph was short-lived.

The front door slammed and Mum's voice shouted angrily up the stairs.

"Katrina! Come down here. I want a word with you!"

It was terrible. Mum had bumped into Daisy's parents in the supermarket.

"How's Katrina?" Daisy's mum had asked innocently. "We haven't seen her for ages."

"Oh really?" Mum had said. She'd pursed her lips, thought for a minute and come straight home, abandoning her trolley in the middle of the aisle.

"What have you been up to?"

Katrina said nothing. She looked at Dad. Dad looked at the floor.

"Where have you *been*?" Mum continued. "All these afternoons after school. You *told* us you were at *Daisy's*. You haven't been there *once*, have you?"

"I did once," said Katrina timidly. *Dived off the landing and fell back up,* she thought, wondering if she should do the same demonstration for Mum.

There was a horrible silence. Mum tapped her foot. Then a thought occurred to her. Katrina could see it enter Mum's mind. There was only one other time that Katrina had deliberately deceived Mum and it had been at the start of the summer holidays. Mum narrowed her eyes suspiciously. "Does this have anything to do with that Merlin character?" she said.

Dad shifted uncomfortably in his seat. He knew Merlin was real. The sorcerer had done a manifestation in front of Dad in the summer and grown thirty feet tall before his eyes. Dad found the only way to cope was to completely ignore the subject. He had pretended that it wasn't happening, that Merlin didn't exist.

But Dad couldn't go on like that for ever. He looked at Katrina nervously. Katrina's eyes told him that Merlin was back and that there was another crisis. Katrina's eyes were silently pleading for help.

Dad took a very deep breath and said, "Actually, Kat's been helping me. That's why she hasn't been at Daisy's."

"What?!" Mum swung round to face him with such force that Dad recoiled and hit his head on the kitchen wall.

"Erm, yes..." said Dad, rubbing his head and staring at the ceiling for inspiration. "She's been helping me ... in the shed ... after school. We've been..."

"Making something?" offered Katrina.

"Yes," agreed Dad quickly. "Making something."

"Making what?" demanded Mum.

"Erm." Dad looked desperately at Katrina.

"Well," Katrina said, sucking in air through her teeth, "it's a surprise."

"Yes!" said Dad. "That's what it is. A surprise. For ... for you!" He smiled brightly at Mum.

"For me?"

"Yes," Katrina leapt in. "For your birthday."

"My birthday isn't for months," Mum growled suspiciously.

"It's going to be a very *big* surprise," said Katrina. "Isn't it Dad?"

"It certainly is," he said, nodding firmly. "A very big surprise indeed."

"Oh." Mum was deflated. "OK then. If that's the case, I suppose I can't say any more about it, can I? I'd better go and finish the shopping." She stumped back down the corridor.

As the front door slammed, Dad looked at Katrina. "I expect you don't want to tell me what's going on," he said, hopefully. "That's OK, I won't ask any questions."

"Actually, Dad," said Katrina sitting down opposite him at the kitchen table and thinking it might be nice to tell someone else what was going on, "I do want to tell you. It's to do with Merlin."

"I'd sort of gathered that," said Dad. "You really don't need to tell me you know."

"I'm a sorceress," continued Katrina, ignoring him. "He's training me."

"Oh," said Dad.

"He's training me in magic because Morgan le Fay wants to kill me."

Katrina didn't need to say any more.

Because suddenly, there she was. Morgan le Fay was standing right next to the kitchen sink, her

eyes gleaming with savage triumph. And – strangely – she was brandishing Katrina's teddy bear.

"I have it," Morgan said. She caressed Bernard's throat with the tip of a long, pointed fingernail, and smiled icily at Katrina. "You will perish, Katrina Picket. Slowly, piece by piece. I shall make sure of that."

There was an eruption of red sparks and Morgan was gone.

"Oh," said Dad.

"Ah," said Katrina.

And they were both silent.

The Love Object

Late as it was, Dad drove Katrina straight round to the Royal Stilton. "I'll think of something to tell Mum," he said in a hoarse whisper. "Just get help. Go on." He dropped her off, and Katrina rushed up to Merlin's room.

"Morgan's been here again," she shouted to Merlin as soon as he opened the door. "In my house! She stole my teddy bear!" Katrina sat down in an armchair. "Why on *earth* did she do that?"

Merlin looked at her. "Morgan has taken something of yours? Something dear to you?"

Katrina nodded. "She's got Bernard."

Merlin was deeply shocked. His eyes took on a helpless, hopeless expression. "She has taken something precious," he said flatly. "She has removed your Love Object. Oh dear."

Before Katrina could open her mouth to say anything, Merlin sighed very deeply, and said with gloomy certainty, "She intends to disembody you. Very nasty. Very nasty indeed. Oh dear…"

Katrina didn't like the sound of that at all.

"Disembody me? What do you mean?"

"Remove you from your body. Strip your soul from you in pieces. It leaves a shell – a living corpse. The essence that is you is blown away with the wind."

Katrina squeaked in a very high voice, "Can I have some tea please?" Hot sweet tea. Mum always made her drink it when she was upset. And she was very upset indeed.

Room service appeared with tea and Katrina sipped some. It steadied her a bit.

"What's Bernard got to do with it?" she said.

Merlin looked very serious. "She has removed

your Love Object. The thing into which you have poured your thoughts, your fears, your hidden longings. It is not a living creature, so your emotions remain trapped and do not flow out again. It contains the essence of you. If she can unlock its secrets, she holds the key to your soul. And then she can steal it from you piece by piece. Dear oh dear."

Katrina was puzzled. She didn't think she had been pouring her soul into Bernard. But then this was all a bit new to her. There was an awful lot to learn.

"I knew her capable of dreadful deeds, Katrinapicket, but this is the worst!" He murmured to himself, so softly that Katrina could barely catch his words, "There is more than sorcerers' rivalry here. This hatred is too particular. To do such a thing to a child!" he exclaimed. "A child… I wonder…" He said no more for a moment. And when he turned to Katrina, he seemed to change the subject. Patting her hand sympathetically, he said, "It is a tragic, *tragic* loss."

"Is it?" she said.

"Yes," said Merlin nodding confidently, "The loss of a Love Object is *devastating*."

"Really?"

"Undoubtedly," said Merlin firmly.

"Well," said Katrina. "It's a bit of a shame. I mean I was quite attached to him. But he was only a cuddly toy. It's not the end of the world, is it?"

"*Isn't* it?"

"No," said Katrina.

The light of hope started to gleam in Merlin's eyes. "You are not crushed and heart sore?"

Katrina thought hard. "No," she answered.

"You do not feel that you have lost a vital part of yourself?"

"Definitely not."

Merlin considered. "Tell me all that has happened with this Bernard since Morgan returned," he said. "Tell me exactly what you have done with him."

Katrina described how she had hung the necklace on him, and how poor Bernard had been incinerated in an instant. How she had hidden the ashes in a drawer so Mum wouldn't find them. How she had restored him as magic practice.

"Aha!" said Merlin with satisfaction. "At last I begin to see!"

"See what?"

"She has been watching you, Katrinapicket, waiting for an opportunity to strike. Think of what she has seen. She sends you a package. It is her first attempt on your life. You have no reason to suspect the necklace is anything but a gift, but you do not adorn yourself as she expected you to, no, you choose to adorn Bernard. And then what is the very first thing you do when you have learnt enough magic? You restore Bernard. Katrinapicket, can you see how it looks to Morgan?"

"Er, no, not really."

"She believes that bear has a *very* special significance for you. That you place Bernard before yourself in importance. She thinks he is a Love Object."

"But it was just coincidence," Katrina said. "I just wanted something to practise on."

"*You* know that. And now *I* know that. But *Morgan* does not." Merlin sat quietly for a moment and then said with barely concealed triumph, "Katrinapicket, I think Morgan has made her first mistake."

Katrina felt hopeful for the first time since

Morgan had appeared by the kitchen sink. She relaxed back into the armchair.

A minute later, she nearly leapt out of her skin. An enormous eye was looking through the window. Something very big and very reptilian was outside.

Aaaaargh! screamed a voice in Katrina's head. *Relax*, she told herself firmly, *calm down*. After all, it shouldn't be that hard to repel a monster. It must be like self-defence, only bigger. She drew up her magic, wrapping it around her, and then – taking a deep breath – she concentrated on trying to force her magical shield outwards like the radiating waves of an explosion. She felt her energy build. It was going to work. It was! She was going to drive off the monster. But before she had a chance, Merlin leapt up, threw open the window and said happily, "Desmond!"

"Desmond!" Katrina echoed, her magic imploding like a deflated balloon. She looked at the eye. The big green eye. The big green friendly eye. A curl of smoke snaked in through the open window.

"Sir Katrinapicket," said Desmond fondly. "Did I scare you?" He smiled cheerfully, revealing his very long, very sharp teeth.

"No," she said. Then, "Well, yes, sorry. Thought you might be Morgan."

Desmond grunted in disgust. The room filled with smoke, the fire alarms went off, and the entire hotel was immediately evacuated.

Outside on Cathedral Green, Katrina hugged Desmond. She had missed him.

Once the fuss had died down, and the firemen had left, the guests were allowed back in. It was very late, and Katrina stifled a yawn.

"Bedtime for you, Katrinapicket," said Merlin. "Take her home, Desmond."

Katrina climbed into the hollow at the base of the dragon's neck. He flexed his wings and with a single, powerful beat, took off smoothly. His claws brushed the treetops that edged Cathedral Green. He kept low, his scaly feet skimming the chimney pots, as he knew Katrina didn't like heights. He landed in Victoria Park, just opposite Katrina's house, gave her a smoky kiss on the cheek and said, "I'll sleep here. Just in case."

Katrina felt much safer, knowing that the dragon was across the road. She fell into bed, and slept a long, dreamless sleep.

The Circus

On Saturday they were all over Bristol – every lamppost, every hoarding, every empty shop. Any space that could carry a poster did.

A photograph of Desmond looking terrifyingly fierce was splashed across the middle.

Cirque de la Lune, it declared. *See the world famous French circus! Amazing animatronics! Appearing in Bristol only, Mordilla – the fire-breathing dragon!*

"Mordilla?" said Katrina. "*Mordilla!*"

"They didn't think 'Desmond' was scary enough," muttered Desmond, an embarrassed flush shimmering across his scales.

"And why does it say 'Bristol only'?" asked Katrina. "Being with a circus could be good, couldn't it? You could travel all over the place with them."

Desmond shook his head firmly. "I was only hitching a lift. I said I'd perform with them if they took me as far as Bristol. I wanted to get back the minute I heard about Morgan. After what she did last time, I thought you might need some help. I tried to fly here but it proved a little tricky. The skies are so full of planes and whatnot, you can hardly move up there these days. And I nearly got shot down by the US air force in New York. Had to make an emergency landing in Central Park. Crashed right next to the circus people's big top as luck would have it. Was surrounded by armed police in an instant. The locals were a little shocked. They'd have had me arrested if the circus lot hadn't covered for me. It was very kind of them. They told the authorities I was their new attraction. And they were heading for Europe right after the New York show, so I came over with them." Desmond smiled at Katrina. "Of course, they'd *like* me to stay on at the circus," he added. "But it would be quite impossible."

"Why?" asked Katrina.

Desmond coughed and shifted uncomfortably. He was going to tell her a deep, dark secret. Katrina leant forward and Desmond looked over his shoulder to check no one could hear. Then he whispered, "They're all – they're all..." He could hardly bring himself to say it. His wings gave a little involuntary flutter. "...*vegetarians!*"

Katrina nodded sympathetically. She could see the problem. No amount of tofu could quite fill the special place in Desmond's stomach where a damsel in distress used to go.

"Oh Desmond," she sighed, patting his claw affectionately. "What are we going to do with you?"

Desmond farted. It was only a little one, but it was enough to tear a bush up by its roots and send it scudding across the park.

"Sorry," said Desmond. "Lentils."

Desmond and Katrina made their way to the Royal Stilton.

"How's your training going?" asked Desmond.

"Oh, well, OK I suppose," Katrina replied.

"I expect you're doing better than that silly Nimue woman Merlin was so infatuated with. She was too stupid to learn *anything*. Never could understand what he saw in her. I bet you're marvellous."

Katrina smiled, grateful for Desmond's encouragement. She didn't like to admit it, but when it came down to it she was terrified. She was trying to carry on as normal – well, as normal as you can be when you're in intensive sorcery training – but the fear sat at the back of her mind and nagged her constantly.

When they reached the hotel, Merlin was still having breakfast, so Katrina and Desmond sat on the grass outside and waited.

"Fancy a game of chess?" Katrina asked him.

She didn't know how to play the game, so Desmond attempted to teach her. He beat her hollow. It cheered him up no end.

"How's the game with Merlin going?" she asked. It seemed to be taking forever. They'd been at it for weeks.

"Ah," said Desmond. "Very complicated." He looked up to check that Merlin hadn't come out yet, and whispered, "I'm winning."

The weather was warm, so Merlin decided they should hold their training session outside. They walked up to the Downs, where the circus people's big top and caravans were roped off from the public. Desmond would be safe from unwelcome attention there, and Merlin could train Katrina in a quiet corner without being pestered.

He'd decided to teach her Voluntary Transformation. Until now, Katrina's bodily changes had been inflicted upon her by Merlin. Now it was time for her to try changing herself.

Desmond curled up around a huge chestnut tree, his stomach rumbling noisily. His huge body shielded Katrina and Merlin from the gaze of passing onlookers.

"Tell me, Katrinapicket," Merlin began, "how does it feel when I transform you?"

"Horrible," said Katrina. "It makes me feel sick."

"Quite so," said Merlin happily. "Because in that instance the magic is externally applied. But now you're going to learn the process in reverse – from the inside out as it were. We'd better start with something small. Is there a creature with which you're particularly familiar?"

Katrina thought hard. They hadn't had any pets at home since Adrian's hamster had escaped and met an unfortunate end in the jaws of next door's cat. It had been the last in a long line of Adrian's pets that had experienced sad and sudden deaths. Mum had declared she couldn't stand any more bloodshed and had refused to allow a single creature in the house since. The animal Katrina was most familiar with was probably their neighbour's dog – a friendly, bouncy Jack Russell terrier called Pippa who Katrina occasionally took for walks.

Katrina nodded at Merlin. "Yes," she said. "There's a dog I know quite well."

"Right then, Katrinapicket. You must give yourself time to think about the shape of this creature. Sit here on the grass. Close your eyes. Now picture the animal."

Katrina did what Merlin told her.

"Draw the creature with your mind's eye: compose it in your head, from the tip of its tail to the end of its nose. Do you see it, Katrinapicket?"

Katrina held Pippa's image in her mind and nodded.

"Now the next part is exceedingly tricky. You must go inside the beast. Take your mind into the animal's body. Inhabit its space – its form – and at the same time draw upon your own magic … slowly, slowly… Now don't shield – you must use the magic to wipe your own body away. Erase the human shape, and leave the dog. Go carefully, Katrinapicket, we don't want any accidents."

Katrina – who had been following the instructions as he spoke them – mentally began to rub away parts of herself. She'd got as far as one arm and her left foot when she was distracted by a particularly noisy rumble from Desmond's stomach.

"Sorry," apologized Desmond.

Katrina opened her eyes.

Mistake. Big, big mistake. Horrified, she looked down at the place where her foot should have been. It was missing. Her leg ended in a messy, blurred stump. The image of the terrier vanished from her mind completely.

"Oh dear," said Merlin.

"My foot's gone!" Katrina squealed. "And my arm! Oh yuck!"

"Keep calm, Katrinapicket," tutted Merlin. "There's no need to panic."

"No need to panic? Bits of me are missing!"

Merlin's tone was stern. "Katrinapicket, you are a sorceress. Small body parts can be put back in a jiffy. Come on. Keep going."

So Katrina sat and shut her eyes once more, composed a Jack Russell in her head and then continued to rub out her own body. It was a laborious process, but this time Katrina's attention didn't waver. She saved her head until last and when she'd wiped it out, she opened her eyes once more. And, from a position uncomfortably near the ground, she looked up at Merlin, barked once, and wagged her tail.

"Oh very well done! Astonishing! Marvellous!" exclaimed Merlin. "That's quite remarkable for a first attempt." He peered at Katrina's fur. "Of course the colour's a little strange, but let's not be picky."

Katrina looked at her paws. They were bright pink. And instead of the black and tan patches that

were a feature of Pippa's fur, Katrina had large dollops of dazzling turquoise. How on earth had that
happened? Before she had time to consider the
problem, she was faced with a rather larger one. A
wandering mongrel had spotted her from across
the Downs and was heading, tail wagging, tongue
lolling, eyes bright with canine curiosity, straight
for her. Katrina – who knew exactly how dogs
greeted each other, and didn't want to be sniffed
anywhere thank-you-very-much – threw all her
attention into restoring herself. An explosion of
pink sparks, a waft of burnt-out fireworks, and she
was back.

The dog yelped, and fled with its tail between its
legs. Once it had gone, Merlin made Katrina keep
practising. "Speed is of the essence," he told her.
"To be of any use at all, Voluntary Transformation
must be instant."

It was a bit like learning to read, thought
Katrina. To start with she had to work on each
individual stage of the process. Then she had to
try to stick all the elements together. It was really
difficult, but eventually she began to speed up. By
lunchtime Katrina could change into a dog in less

than two seconds. It was only then that Merlin allowed her to rest.

She sat, leaning against Desmond's sun-warmed scales.

"Fantastic," Desmond said fondly. "Well done."

"Thanks," she said, smiling. "Pity about the colour." Try as she might, she hadn't managed anything but bright pink fur with turquoise patches.

"Never mind," said Desmond kindly. "I thought it was rather fetching."

Katrina sat, thoughtfully chewing the now squashed sandwich that Dad had given her that morning. It was all very well mastering a new skill but when it came down to it, what use was a pink Jack Russell going to be against Morgan le Fay?

A little later, they all walked to the edge of the Downs. Merlin and Desmond were admiring the view of the gorge. Katrina was keeping well back from the edge, looking at the suspension bridge and trying not to let her eyes be drawn by the ghastly drop below it. Something flashed at the far side of the bridge. There was a glint of metal. For a moment Katrina felt as if the air had been punched out of her.

They were a long way away, but they were unmistakable. Coming towards them over the bridge, three abreast, rode a column of knights in shining armour.

Tears sprang in Katrina's eyes and fresh courage swelled in her chest. "He's back!" she gasped, pulling Merlin by the sleeve. "Oh Merlin! Arthur's come back!"

Katrina's heart pounded painfully and her cheeks flushed hot with confused excitement. She was so preoccupied with getting her own emotions under control that she didn't notice Merlin's expression.

His face was grey with fear.

Merlin's Vision

Katrina sprinted across the grass and then screeched to a halt when she reached the bridge. Nothing was going to make her set foot on that walkway again. She waited on solid land while the knights rode towards her.

When Arthur spotted Katrina, he smiled, a rich warm grin of happiness that seemed to melt Katrina's knees completely.

"Well met, Sir Katrinapicket," he said, reaching down from his horse. Katrina thought he would simply clasp her arm in greeting – the knights seemed to go in for a lot of arm clasping when they were saying hello to each other. She extended an arm towards Arthur and was astonished to find herself hoisted bodily into the air and then swung across his horse's neck. They rode towards Merlin and Desmond with Katrina sitting in front of King Arthur, astride his charger, blushing deep, hot scarlet.

Desmond led everyone to the circus camp and ushered them all in through the public barrier like an over anxious teacher on a school trip. None of the circus performers batted an eyelid at the sudden addition of 149 knights in shining armour to their troupe. Arthur and his comrades were greeted as if they were fellow travellers – a jovial smile here, a friendly pat on the back there – and then they were left to their own devices.

Once they were safely inside the camp there was time to greet everyone properly. It seemed that the knights had dispersed across the globe during the summer. Some had gone to America with King Arthur, others had ended up in various theme parks. Many – like Sir Gawain and his brothers – had found jobs performing extraordinarily realistic jousting displays at castles across Europe. But each had immediately responded to Arthur's call, and they were all joyfully excited to be together once more. The mood was contagious and yet Merlin looked upon the gathered knights with sick dread in his eyes.

An hour later, Katrina and Merlin were in the supermarket, filling a line of trolleys with food for all the knights. Every one of them had made a long journey and they were very hungry.

"How much bread should we get?" Katrina wondered aloud. "If they eat about a quarter of a loaf each that would be enough, wouldn't it? How many loaves does that make? I wish I wasn't so bad at sums."

Merlin didn't worry about the maths. He simply piled loaf after loaf into a trolley until it was full. "That'll do," he said flatly.

"Did you know that they would all come back?" Katrina asked Merlin.

"I suppose if I'd *thought* about it, I could have predicted it," said Merlin. "Honourable types, you see. All of them. They wouldn't let you face Morgan alone. More's the pity." He swept a shelf

full of tins into another trolley, not much minding if they went in or not. Several cans spun across the floor and disappeared under shelves. He heaved a gloomy sigh.

It was then that Katrina looked at Merlin properly, and took in his mood of dark despair. Her joy at Arthur's arrival was instantly swallowed up by fear as she remembered Merlin's vision. Katrina gulped nervously.

"It's that vision, isn't it?" she said. "You think it showed the future, not the past."

"It seems possible," conceded Merlin. "While they were all safely away I knew it couldn't happen. But now…"

The sentence hung, unfinished, in the air.

Yes, thought Katrina. *Now they're all back. That's the problem. They're good, and kind and honourable, so they came back to help me. And now they've played right into Morgan's hands and it's all my fault.* For a moment Katrina was so chilled with horror she thought she might be sick. Then she remembered how Merlin hadn't quite met her eyes after he'd had the vision and a new, dreadful thought occurred to her. "When you saw them dead," she

101

asked, in a hoarse whisper, "was I there, too?"

Merlin didn't say a word, but the agonized look he gave Katrina told her all she needed to know.

"No one in the kingdom of Albion shall escape the suffering to come," Merlin said softly. "My inner eye foresaw it all last time, you know, when Arthur was on the throne. A bloody battle, the whole kingdom destroyed. Good people – innocent bystanders – murdered for her pleasure. And I couldn't bear to watch. That's why I put myself to sleep in the cave. Do you blame me?"

Katrina didn't. If she knew how to do it, she'd be tempted to do exactly the same thing. But she didn't. She was going to have to watch them die. All of them. One by one. King Arthur, Lancelot, Guinevere, 149 knights, Mum, Dad, Adrian, Daisy … Desmond. Or maybe she'd be lucky. Maybe Morgan would kill her first. Katrina closed her eyes to stop the tears from welling up.

But then a switch flicked in Katrina's brain. "Merlin, what would have happened last time if you'd stayed awake – if you hadn't gone to sleep in that cave?" she asked urgently. "Could you have changed things?"

Merlin shook his head firmly. "No, Katrinapicket. I could change nothing. Why else would I have despaired? I saw a future that was certain."

"How do you know?"

Merlin shrugged helplessly. "I searched my inner eye. Over and over again I looked. Each time it was the same: death, devastation, horror, unbearable grief." His hand went to his face as if he wanted to wipe away the memory of it.

Katrina tugged at his sleeve insistently. "But this summer you had a vision too – do you remember? When Arthur was going to challenge the Queen. You saw them dead then, shot by her bodyguards. But that didn't happen because we *changed* it. We changed the future. Can't we do that now?"

Merlin looked at Katrina as if a possibility had opened up that he'd never seen before. "You may be right..." he said slowly. "You may be... Good heavens!"

"Maybe all the bad things happened last time *because* you weren't there to stop them. Believing they would happen *made* them happen—"

Katrina couldn't say any more, because suddenly she was swamped by Merlin's beard as he enveloped her in a huge, hopeful hug.

"Katrinapicket," Merlin said in a muffled sort of way. "Katrinapicket, if you are right, you are indeed a marvel!"

Figments of the Imagination

They paid for the shopping with Merlin's dwindling supply of cash, and then loaded up Desmond, who had been waiting patiently in the car park. They piled carrier bags into the hollow at the base of his neck until it was full. Desmond carried the remainder in his mouth, the bulging bags suspended from his long, sharp teeth like lumpen balloons.

The feast took place on the grass beside the circus caravans in the fading autumn sunshine.

Merlin and Katrina had bought the entire contents of the supermarket meat cabinet for Desmond, but it still wasn't enough. He sat watching the knights eat, his stomach rumbling noisily, until the circus ringmaster called him in to the big top for his matinee performance.

Katrina sat near Sir Gawain and his brothers. They were funny and lively and serious and warm-hearted. King Arthur smiled across at her, and Katrina thought that whatever happened next, with these knights beside her, she could cope with anything.

Well, almost anything.

Before they had finished eating, there was a shower of red sparks, and Morgan appeared in the middle of them, radiating evil with such repellent force that it threw them all on to their backs.

She hurled Bernard – the blackened and charred teddy – into Katrina's lap.

"You have tricked me," Morgan hissed. "You will pay for that Katrina Picket. You will *all* pay." Her eyes slid, serpent-like, across the faces of the assembled knights until she found Arthur's. "You will be destroyed once more, my brother. I shall lay waste the kingdom of Albion."

Morgan disappeared before Merlin or Katrina could do anything.

The sky darkened suddenly, and the warm afternoon turned icy cold. Thick red mist rolled across the Downs. There was a moment's silence and then the sound of slow, heavy footsteps coming closer and closer.

Arthur and his knights got to their feet, pulling swords from scabbards in readiness for battle.

Katrina stood, looking frantically through the mist to see who – or what – was coming for them. But then Merlin was at her side. "Don't turn round," he told her. "And whatever happens, do not look upon the face of your attacker. If you do so, you are lost."

Katrina tried not to look but she couldn't avoid seeing what was happening around her. Out of the mist an army appeared, advancing slowly towards the knights. They were surrounded. Katrina watched them approach, fighting the urge to run.

It was the strangest army Katrina had ever seen.

A huge man entirely dressed in green stepped forward and Katrina saw – to her surprise – that his hair and skin were as green as his tunic. Sir Gawain was standing beside Katrina. At her gasp, he turned, looked straight at the green knight, and gave a dismayed cry of recognition. Gawain tightened his grip on his sword and prepared to fight.

Beside the green knight a strange animal approached bounding across the grass in great, eratic leaps. Its vast serpent's head was joined to a body that was spotted and furry like a leopard's for half its length but finished in the hind quarters and tail of a lion.

"What is it?" Katrina asked in a horrified whisper.

"The Questing Beast," replied Merlin.

The creature started to make a peculiar, unearthly noise – almost like a pack of yelping dogs – and immediately a knight to the left of Katrina let out a despairing roar, turned and chased after it.

"He is doomed to follow," Merlin sighed. "Always to chase, but never to catch it."

Sure enough, as soon as the knight got within striking distance, the beast disappeared. Then it popped its head round a tree fifty metres away. The knight chased it, but as soon as he got close, the beast disappeared again. It was leading the knight in an exhausting game of hide and seek across the Downs.

Katrina's heart jolted with terror. Mordred was advancing on Arthur.

But Desmond ate him, thought Katrina. *He should be a pile of dragon dung. What's he doing here?*

"Love *you*?" Mordred was saying in his sneering, slimy voice as he came towards Arthur. "Guinevere doesn't love *you*. She's pretending. She may have married you, Arthur, but it's *Lancelot* she really loves."

Katrina looked across at Lancelot.

Another Mordred was advancing on him, taunting him, "Call yourself an *honourable* man? In love with your best friend's *wife!*"

She looked at Guinevere. She, too, was facing yet another Mordred.

"In love with *two* men, my lady?" the third Mordred sneered. "That's not *allowed*."

Three Mordreds? How could there be three Mordreds?

"They're not real are they?" Katrina asked Merlin.

"No, they're not. Whole blessed army is a bunch of figments."

"What's a figment?"

"It takes its shape from the mind of its opponent. Finds your weakest point and uses it. The knights are facing enemies of their own invention – their own demons, if you like."

"But if they're not real, they can't hurt, can they?"

"Oh yes they can," said Merlin. "Worse than a real enemy. They know exactly where to hit."

Katrina couldn't begin to imagine what was coming through the mist for her, but she was sure it would involve a great height and a very long fall.

"What do we do?" she said urgently.

"Go round the problem, Katrinapicket. Do what Morgan does not expect. We cannot meet her head on. But there are two of us. Let us transform – something small, I think. Perhaps we can slip past Morgan's army. Once we are out of this enchanted circle we can think what to do."

But just as he finished his sentence, they heard a voice. Soft, feminine and delicate. An enchanting voice, it was calling Merlin's name.

"Merlin! Merlin! My love…"

The effect was astonishing. Merlin's hand went to his heart. He blushed to the roots of his hair. His mouth opened and closed for a few moments before he could get any words out. When he spoke, it was in a trembling whisper.

"Oh my goodness!" he muttered in confused delight. "Is it really…? Can it be…?" And before Katrina could stop him, he had turned to look.

"Nimue!" gushed Merlin. "Nimue! Oh, my love!"

Katrina couldn't help it. She had to look.

Merlin had fallen to his knees and was gazing in rapt adoration at the woman who approached.

She was beautiful – more beautiful than anyone Katrina had ever seen. But it was not a human beauty. Katrina noticed that Nimue moved in an extraordinary way; she wasn't walking towards Merlin, it was more like gliding. Well, no, not even gliding. She was *flowing* towards him – like an incoming tide.

The sorcerer was going to be washed away.

"Merlin," Nimue breathed, caressing his head and lifting his chin so that their eyes met. "Oh Merlin, how I've missed you."

111

He was lost. Katrina knew that Merlin was totally unaware of anything else. The battle with Morgan, the figments... The world could cease to exist and Merlin wouldn't notice. He was drowning in the limpid depths of Nimue's eyes.

Katrina looked around desperately for help. Arthur had his sword drawn and was advancing on his Mordred.

"Not this time," Arthur was saying. "You'll not twist everything this time. Leave us be!"

Lancelot was already locked in mortal combat with Mordred 2, and Guinevere was fighting Mordred 3. She was very good with a sword, Katrina noticed.

"They're figments!" Katrina shouted. "They're not real!"

Her words were lost. No one could hear her. They were all gripped in deadly battle with their own personal horrors. Katrina tried to keep a firm hold on the glimmer of hope that she'd ignited in the supermarket. This didn't have to end in disaster. She *could* change the future. It *was* possible. But – Katrina thought despairingly – no amount of hope could alter the fact that she was going to have to fight a fiendishly powerful sorceress.

As Katrina stood in the midst of the battle she became puzzled. No figment had come for her.

And then Katrina realized with sickening certainty that Morgan had sent the figments as a diversion to keep the knights occupied – a way of ensuring that Katrina was entirely unprotected.

She was utterly alone.

What was Morgan going to do now?

A screaming bellow echoed across the Downs, a roar of pain, the anguished cry of an animal in distress.

A very large animal in very deep distress.

"Desmond!" Katrina cried. Morgan was doing something terrible to Desmond.

Without thinking, she ran. Through the caravans, across the grass and into the big top.

Straight into Morgan's trap.

The Big Top

A strange scene was taking place.

Desmond was chained by the neck in the corner of the big top between two banks of seats.

Morgan was in the circus ring in front of him, just out of his reach. Only she didn't look the same. She was dressed in a theatrical costume – a flowing medieval dress and pointy hat with a long veil. A damsel in distress.

Poor Desmond couldn't bear it.

Morgan prowled up and down, just out of reach,

saying, "Feeling peckish *Mordilla*? Oh, what a tasty morsel I am. Yum, yum."

Desmond – hungry, desperate Desmond – bellowed in an agony of starved frustration.

The crowd roared with laughter. The big top was packed to bursting with an audience who thought Desmond was a superb high-tech special effect and the whole scene was gloriously comic. They had no idea they were in mortal danger.

Katrina watched Desmond as a big dragon tear squeezed out of one eye, rolled down his scaly nose and plopped on to the sawdust of the ring floor.

"Desmond!" Katrina's heart contracted in sympathy and she marched furiously up to Morgan.

"You– you– you–COW!" Katrina shouted.

Morgan looked at Katrina. Her eyes were cold, but the glint of triumph in them was unmistakable.

That was exactly what she expected me to do, thought Katrina. *Oh dear*. She hadn't gone round the problem at all. She had met it head on. Did being blasted to bits come next?

Morgan pulled off her pointy hat and raised an eyebrow.

"Katrina Picket, how very predictable you are.

It's disappointing, really. I should have enjoyed rather more of a battle."

Katrina had no idea what to do, so she did the first thing that came into her head – she transformed. She found her inner Jack Russell and wiped away the rest of her body. Katrina noted that her speed was improving – it had taken less than a second. The crowd burst into spontaneous applause.

Katrina did what Jack Russells do best – she sank her teeth into Morgan's ankle. Morgan didn't even flinch. Katrina growled and tugged and shook with all her might, but Morgan simply laughed at her. She lifted Katrina by the scruff of her neck and their eyes connected. "Call that a transformation? Pathetic! *This* is a transformation."

And Katrina found herself held in the claws of a huge, horned bear with razor sharp teeth – the creature from a nightmare.

A dim memory sparked in Katrina's head. She'd seen a wizard duel in a cartoon once. Both wizards had kept changing into different animals. But the winning wizard had turned himself into a germ. That was it! A germ!

Quickly Katrina formed the image of a germ

deep inside. She exploded her inner dog and took the new form.

It wasn't quite the effect she'd hoped for. The trouble was, Katrina had no idea what a germ looked like. She'd pictured something small and blobby. What she actually turned into was a large pink bogey that was stuck fast to Morgan-the-horned-bear's claw.

It bought her a little time. While Morgan tried to scrape Katrina-the-bogey off, Katrina was telling herself, *Think! Think! Do what she won't expect...*

Morgan flicked Katrina-the-bogey across the circus ring. Katrina transformed back into her own body in mid-air.

And then she did exactly what Morgan wouldn't expect.

Katrina Picket was terrified of heights.

So she began to climb.

Up and up Katrina climbed, clinging to the rigging of the big top until she came to a platform. The Flying Fandangos – a troupe of French trapeze artists in spangly costumes – were already there, waiting to begin their act.

One of the Flying Fandangos had slipped on the

steps of their caravan earlier that day and sprained an ankle, so a student from Bristol's circus school had volunteered to fill the gap. But at that moment the nervous student was trapped inside a toilet, wrestling with the faulty lock on a Portaloo door. In the blinding glare of the spotlights Katrina looked like any other performer.

"Bonsoir!" A small dark man with a very large moustache slapped Katrina on the back.

"Bon what?" she said, looking down and wishing she hadn't.

"Tu es prêt?"

"Pardon?"

Before Katrina had time to think, or do anything, the man climbed on to his trapeze, dangled upside down and, to her horror, grabbed Katrina's hands and launched them both into space.

"Waaaaaaaaaah!" she screamed as they swung across the big top and, "Woooooooooooh!" she cried as they swung back again.

Well Morgan certainly won't be expecting this, Katrina thought as she swung backwards and forwards across the circus tent.

The man gave her a tremendous heave and then

let go. Katrina soared through the air and a second trapeze artist grabbed her by the legs.

Predictable huh? she thought, upside down, the blood rushing to her head. *We'll see about that.*

Another heave and she flew through the air looking ungainly and undignified, the French man just catching her by one ankle. The crowd below were in fits of giggles.

The man threw Katrina again, and this time, surprisingly, she ended up the right way round. *That's better*, she thought, looking up to see who had caught her. But instead of the friendly face of the trapeze artist, she looked straight into the cold eyes of Morgan le Fay.

"I'm not so easy to evade," said the sorceress as they swung through the air.

Even through her terror, Katrina realized that Morgan was finding it hard to maintain a grip on her. The air itself seemed to struggle to force them apart like the opposing poles of a magnet.

Katrina made use of it. As the second, empty trapeze flew past she kicked her legs out and hooked a knee over the pole. She was ripped from Morgan's grasp.

But then Morgan started her attack.

She hurled thunderbolts and wintry gales at Katrina. She pelted her with snow and hail. The crowd below marvelled at the extraordinary display of weather conditions that raged inside the tent.

Even upside down and swinging wildly through the air Katrina managed to deflect Morgan's elementals. But all Katrina was doing was self-defence. She couldn't begin to fight back. Morgan's powers seemed limitless, and Katrina was getting tired. She knew she wouldn't be able to keep it up for ever. As soon as this doubt entered her mind, Katrina's shield weakened a little. A small chink appeared in her defences. Morgan sensed it and threw a Transforming blast at her.

Most of it dripped harmlessly off. Most, but not all. Katrina looked up to see a gigantic pair of yellow duck feet attached to the end of her legs. The sight was so distracting that she lost her concentration completely and Morgan made her move. She blocked Katrina's powers – piercing her, cracking the glassy pool of magic deep inside her, shattering it completely.

Katrina felt it go. She was exposed. Helpless. But she wasn't going to give up.

Go around the problem, she told herself. *Do something she doesn't expect.*

Katrina Picket was terrified of falling.

So she let go of the trapeze.

Katrina dived, headfirst towards the circus floor.

She had no plan. There was nothing she could do. Morgan had blocked her. She was going to die. But at least she wouldn't give Morgan the pleasure of killing her.

The crowd will enjoy this, she thought as she hurtled past the blurred faces. She knew that there was no point even trying to summon Merlin – he was lost to everything but Nimue.

Oh well, she thought sadly. *I tried. At least I won't have to watch all the others get killed.*

The ground rushed to meet her. She shut her eyes.

Katrina hit something.

Something springy.

She brushed her nose on the sawdust and was thrown back up, soaring into the air with breathtaking speed. She'd hit the safety net!

"Wooooooooooh!" she screamed as she flew up.

Morgan was still on the trapeze, hanging motionless in the centre of the big top. She had stopped swinging to watch Katrina die but as Katrina flew up to meet her, she struggled to pull herself upright. Morgan looked scared. More than that. She looked terrified.

Katrina was heading straight for Morgan's trapeze. She was just underneath it. She was level with it...

Katrina didn't even think about blasting Morgan with magic. Instead, she swung her right arm and unleashed a bone-cracking thump on Morgan's jaw. Morgan lost her balance. She fell.

At that moment, Katrina felt her powers flood back – Morgan had lost the magical grip on her.

Katrina flew up for another metre or so, turned and landed gently on the trapeze, where – once she'd restored her own feet to the ends of her legs – she sat looking elegant and unruffled.

Morgan was still falling, but for how much longer? Merlin had warned Katrina not to even attempt to block Morgan's powers but what choice did she have? Katrina concentrated. She focussed.

Mentally unwrapped the shield she'd held around herself and formed it into a sharp point. And then Katrina hurled every last scrap of her magical energy towards Morgan like an invisible spear.

It worked. Katrina pierced the infinite blackness of Morgan's soul and for a moment she was sucked into terrifying darkness. But then she heard Desmond's roar, and with an almighty effort Katrina tore herself away from the touch of Morgan's core, reaching desperately for her own body before she drowned in endless night.

The air was split by a shriek of rage. Morgan couldn't save herself!

With a deafening bellow, Desmond pulled free of his chain and ripped away the safety net. Morgan landed – *plop!* – in Desmond's open mouth.

There was an astonished gasp from the crowd and a moment of hushed silence. Then Desmond stepped forward, burped loudly and said with satisfaction, "Damsel in distress. My favourite."

The crowd was ecstatic – clapping and whooping with delight.

A plume of red smoke curled from Desmond's

126

ear when he swallowed. Katrina watched it drift through the entrance of the big top and away into the darkness.

"She's gone," whispered Katrina, and an immense, overwhelming wave of weariness swept over her.

The brush against Morgan's black soul had dizzied her. Sitting on the trapeze high above the crowd, Katrina suddenly felt horribly sick. And then she fainted, slipping quietly off the trapeze and falling towards the ring.

No one noticed. No one saw.

No one but Desmond.

A crack of leathery wings, and Desmond caught Katrina in mid-air. With a breath of fire from his nostrils, he blew a hole in the big top's roof and flew through it, carrying the unconscious Katrina into the clear cool air.

The crowd cheered. They stood up in their seats and whistled in appreciation.

"Bravo!" they shouted. "Fantastic! What a finale!"

* * *

Katrina revived as soon as they landed on the battle-field. With Morgan gone, the figments had vanished too, but the wounds they had inflicted remained. It was a terrible scene. Katrina looked at the bodies scattered motionless across the Downs and felt despair settle heavily upon her. She may have saved the people of Albion from Morgan, but she'd done nothing to save the Knights of the Round Table.

Guinevere was lying on the ground with Arthur and Lancelot beside her, each holding one of her hands. They were as still as death. Merlin was nowhere to be seen.

Katrina stared in horror until Desmond prodded her in the back.

"Go on," he said. "Do your stuff."

"What can I do?" she said, exhausted and confused. "Shall I call an ambulance? I don't know any first aid."

"First aid?" he said. "*First aid*? You can heal them without first aid. You're a *sorceress*!"

"Oh," said Katrina. "Oh, I *see*."

After all, she'd mended a hole in the hotel wall and she'd put Bernard back together. Healing should work in the same way as Restoration, shouldn't it?

Katrina concentrated. She dipped into the cool calm of her inner source of magic, and it refreshed her.

Katrina sprinkled Guinevere with pink sparks. To her immense relief, Guinevere stirred, opened her eyes, and smiled gratefully. Then Katrina revived Arthur and Lancelot, and sealed the rather nasty gash that ran across the back of Gawain's neck. She found the exhausted knight who had been chasing the strange looking Questing Beast and repaired his blistered feet. She walked around the battlefield showering knights in pink sparks, restoring consciousness and healing wounds.

The only one she couldn't help was Merlin. She found him eventually, hiding behind a tree, blushing and rubbing his chest. Sorrowfully he said, "Oh, my poor heart, Katrinapicket. It is sore. Sore indeed."

Katrina had an idea. She sprinted all the way to the nearest corner shop, and then ran back clutching the stitch in her side with one hand and a small paper bag in the other.

"Here," she said breathlessly, handing Merlin the bag. "Eat this. It might help."

Merlin looked into the bag and smiled a brave smile. He pulled the jar out and began to scoop marmalade into his mouth with his finger.

Suddenly there was an enormous explosion and the tree Merlin had been hiding behind was ripped up by its roots. Katrina looked round in surprise.

"Pardon me," said Desmond. "Touch of wind. Sorry."

"Desmond," said Merlin sternly. "You didn't *eat* her did you?"

Desmond looked at the grass, and then at Merlin. Slowly, he nodded his head.

"Oh *Desmond*," said Merlin horrified. "You silly, silly dragon. It's not *Wednesday*."

Wind Damage

B ristol experienced severe localized storms that
night. The circus performers hitched up their
caravans and drove off the minute Merlin warned
them of what was to come. But the residents of the
area around the Downs couldn't get away and
took the full force of Desmond's intestinal problems. His wind ripped the tiles off the roofs of
elegant houses, felled carefully pruned trees and
overturned expensive cars.

Startled patients in the local hospital lay in their

beds and watched as the ceiling was peeled off by the high wind. They had an extraordinary view of the night sky before the big top – whose ropes had snapped under the extreme pressure – was torn from the ground and deposited on top of the hospital, giving them a colourful new roof.

There was nothing anyone could do for Desmond.

"We can't even attempt to heal his tummy ache at the moment," yelled Merlin. "If we send sparks out in this wind they'll blow around all over the place. Could cause terrible damage. We'll just have to leave him to it."

Katrina, Merlin, Arthur, Lancelot, Guinevere and the knights in shining armour left their horses huddling nervously on Cathedral Green and took refuge in the penthouse of the Royal Stilton. It was just as well it was so big.

After a small feast of toasted sandwiches – the best that room service could offer at this late hour – Arthur, Lancelot, Guinevere and the knights lay down wherever they could find some space and slept.

Katrina and Merlin sat outside in the corridor for

a while and talked.

"Desmond will be all right, won't he?" asked Katrina anxiously.

"I hope so, Katrinapicket. He's a strong fellow. But it's really not good for a dragon to eat anyone unless it's Wednesday. Desmond's old enough to know better. It's not even as if she was a real human being. Who knows what the effects will be? Still, not much we can do for him until his wind dies down."

Katrina remembered the plume of red smoke that had escaped from Desmond's ear.

"She didn't die, did she?" said Katrina.

"No, indeed not. She had created a temporary body for herself. Disposable, you know? The essence of her remains in the world. But I doubt she'll return to Albion. She won't try tackling you again, that's for certain."

Katrina thought of the safety net, and the look of terror on Morgan's face when she had bounced back up.

"Why was Morgan so scared?" she asked.

Merlin scratched his head. "Well, Katrinapicket, I don't think she knew about the safety net. She blocked you. You let go. You should have fallen to the ground, but you didn't. And now she believes that your powers can't be blocked and that you're more powerful than her. And you're only eleven, remember, and she's as old as time itself. No wonder she was scared."

"I'm not, though, am I?" said Katrina. "It was just an accident. I didn't know about the net either."

"But what is an accident, Katrinapicket? You reacted on instinct. Inspiration. Who knows quite where it comes from? And you succeeded in blocking her – you actually managed to shatter her core for a moment. That was extraordinary – remarkable. You are strong in ways that I confess I had not properly understood. Morgan has good cause to fear you."

Katrina sighed. "I still don't get it," she said. "I mean, is that really the only reason she wanted to get rid of me?"

"She's a bully," Merlin said, shaking his head ruefully. "And, of course, it is her nature to hate. But I can't help wondering…"

"What?" said Katrina.

Merlin looked around to check that no one was

listening, leant forward and then said in a very hushed whisper, "Everyone thinks that Guinevere was childless. That's what most of the books will tell you. But it isn't true."

"Really?" Katrina whispered back.

Merlin nodded.

"She had a baby; a little girl. I warned her to conceal the child – send her far away. I knew the baby wouldn't be safe, you see, if Morgan found out. So that's what Guinevere did. It broke her heart, but she did it – for the sake of her child. And I can't help wondering if you are descended from that baby. I didn't dare mention it before in case Morgan heard me. But I think that somehow she sensed it."

Katrina was struggling to take it in. "So that means Arthur's my sort of great grandfather?"

Merlin coughed, blushed very pink. "Well, yes, I think so … probably."

Katrina's eyes widened. "Oh… You mean it might be Lancelot?"

"Maybe. I don't know. I don't think anyone knows. Anyway, the point is that there *is* something special about you. Desmond noticed it too, if you remember, the first time he saw you."

They both thought of Desmond, lying on the Downs in agony.

"I hope he's OK," said Katrina.

"Oh indeed," said Merlin. "And let us hope there are no lasting ill effects."

As they talked on, the wind seemed to die down a little. Katrina and Merlin slept at last – curling up on the luxuriously thick carpet along with everyone else. When they woke it was calm outside. Katrina, Merlin and a long column of knights went to check on Desmond.

Katrina barely recognized the Downs. There wasn't a tree, bush or plant left standing. Even the grass had been peeled away and lay curled at the edge of the gorge like gigantic rolls of carpet.

At the centre of the destruction Desmond lay on the bare earth, looking very tired and rather pale.

"Terribly sorry about all this." He waved a claw at the fallen trees. "Made a bit of a mess."

"Not to worry," said Merlin briskly. "We can put that right in a jiffy."

Arthur and his knights started on the grass – unrolling the vast curls of turf and stamping them back into position. Meanwhile Merlin wandered off to replant trees and shrubs.

Katrina sat with Desmond and stroked his nose. "Are you all right?" she asked. "Is there anything I can do to help?"

"No, no, I shall be fine now," he said wearily. "But if I ever try to eat someone on Saturday again, just stop me. Mind you," he continued sadly, "I think it's put me off a bit. Don't fancy the thought of eating anyone for a very long time. Perhaps I never will."

Katrina thought that it might not be a bad thing if Desmond was put off eating people, even on Wednesdays, but she said nothing.

"You did it then," said Desmond, changing the subject. "Beat Morgan. Knew you could."

Katrina held Desmond's claw and gave it a squeeze. "Thank you," she said.

When he had finished with the vegetation, and the Downs were restored to their former glory, Merlin declared it was time for breakfast.

He shot purple sparks from his fingertips and a round table – *the* Round Table, Katrina realized with a jolt – appeared.

It was a very strange sort of table. It looked no bigger than the one in the kitchen at home. But Arthur, Guinevere, Lancelot, Merlin and the knights could sit around with enough elbow room for a really good feast.

There was one empty seat. *Mordred's*, thought Katrina.

But to her surprise, Arthur pulled it out, and said in his deep, warm voice, "The time has come for you to take your place."

When she approached the chair she could see the words "Sir Katrinapicket" emblazoned across the back in gold.

She sat and a rousing cheer rang through the early morning air. Arthur smiled at her, and Katrina was glad she was sitting down – her legs had failed her again.

And then Guinevere was standing beside her. Holding a goblet high in the air she declared, "A toast! Let us drink to Sir Katrinapicket. For she is as brave as she is beautiful." Guinevere looked

straight at Katrina and her voice dropped so low that the next thing she said reached only Katrina's ears. "A bold knight and a great sorceress: you are truly a queen amongst women. Any mother would be proud indeed to call you her own." Guinevere held Katrina's gaze for a moment longer before smiling warmly and turning to address the knights once more.

"May we stand beside Sir Katrinapicket as long as we have breath in our bodies and blood in our veins!"

"Welcome to the fellowship!" the knights chorused.

Katrina beamed, but found she could say nothing.

At last it was time for Katrina to go home. After all, she had school the next day. There was homework to catch up on. And a surprise to think up for Mum's birthday. It was going to have to be something good...

Dad was alone in the kitchen when Katrina returned, looking pale and anxious. When he saw Katrina he hugged her until he had almost squeezed the breath from her body.

"Has she gone?" he asked.

Katrina nodded.

"You're safe?"

She nodded again.

"Thank heavens!" Dad was silent for a moment, but then, so quietly that Katrina only just caught the words, he said, "And Katrina ... next time you see him, thank Merlin."

When she was ten years old, Katrina Picket woke Merlin.

It was quite by accident – she'd had no intention of doing any such thing. But it was fortunate for everyone in England that she did. They didn't know, of course. The whole thing had to be hushed up. Most people thought it was a particularly inventive party for the Queen's jubilee. And as for the dragon and the exploding fireball – they were explained away as impressive special effects.

But Katrina, and the Prime Minister, knew different…

"Fast-moving fun." *The Scotsman*

**If you've enjoyed reading this book,
look out for...**

Short novels for fluent readers